ARTIVITIES: EXPLORING INNER & OUTER WORLDS THROUGH ART

Artivities encourage exploration of both personal experiences and broader world perspectives through the engaging power of art. It is based on the artist Shilpa Gupta's original "artivity" sheets and her inflatable sculpture *Untitled* (2023). This new iteration has been developed collaboratively by Shilpa Gupta and therapist Rosie McGowan.

The following illustrated pages invite young minds to interact and navigate through complex emotions and reactions to conflict and other challenges. Thoughtfully designed, they engage children, parents, caregivers and teachers in a shared exploration of creativity, empathy and understanding.

The artivities align with *Untitled* (2023), the latest work commissioned for Ng Teng Fong Roof Garden Series at National Gallery Singapore, and reflect Gupta's overall artistic practice. To discover more about the artist's creative process, visit her website: https://shilpagupta.com/

T0302629

4

ARTIVITIES:

EXPLORING INNER & OUTER WORLDS THROUGH ART

BY *SHILPA GUPTA*
WITH *ROSIE MCGOWAN*

Published in 2023

Please direct all enquiries to the publisher at:
National Gallery Singapore
1 St Andrew's Road
#01-01
Singapore 178957

Project Editor: Lam Yong Ling
Managing Editor: Ong Zhen Min
Design Direction: Shilpa Gupta
Designer: FACTORY

Printed in Singapore

The artist would like to thank Pooja Tilve and Nidhi Goel for their valuable inputs on design and editorial content.

All images on pages 56–59 are courtesy of the artist.

Series Partner

Dear Friend,

Let's explore together, through the world of art, our different and sometimes confusing emotions.

You can colour, draw, paste or write on these pages on your own or in a group.

If you are a parent or caregiver, we encourage you to share these artivities with your family. If you are a teacher, we encourage you to take them into your classrooms. There are some suggestions and resources at the back of the book that may help to deepen your explorations.

We look forward to having you join us on this journey.

SHILPA & ROSIE

9

The sixth Ng Teng Fong Roof Garden Commission at National Gallery Singapore is by leading contemporary Indian artist Shilpa Gupta (b. 1976). Her new site-specific work *Untitled* (2023) intrigues us by presenting a classical-looking figurative sculpture, which is not only teasingly fabricated as a large buoyant inflatable, but also shows two seemingly interlocked and combating bodies with upturned limbs that confoundingly rest just on a single head. The surprise is only revealed when one walks around the work.

Walking, exploring, touching, interacting, introspecting, are in fact other intangible but important aspects of Gupta's work because the sculpture is asking to be read in open-ended, multi-faceted ways. For some, the sculpture could represent the deep and enduring sociopolitical problems and tensions of the world. For others, the work surfaces the interpersonal conflicts, psychological dualities, emotional fragilities and mental struggles that we experience daily in our lives.

Untitled (2023) is as family friendly as it is thought-provoking. Gupta's sculpture seeks to appeal in the present worlds of play and gaming for our children and the young-at-heart. But at the same time, it does not neglect the necessary inner work, understanding and transformation within the individual that can follow from one's further engagement with an artwork. As such, Gupta's custom-designed worksheets in this publication, conceptualised in collaboration with therapist Rosie McGowan to accompany this commissioned artwork, is also integral to the experience of Gupta's art. Inspired by Gupta's previous project titled *Artivities*, and her interest in the socio-psychological inquiries of artmaking, this book serves as a tool and resource for participants to embark on a personal journey through art.

11

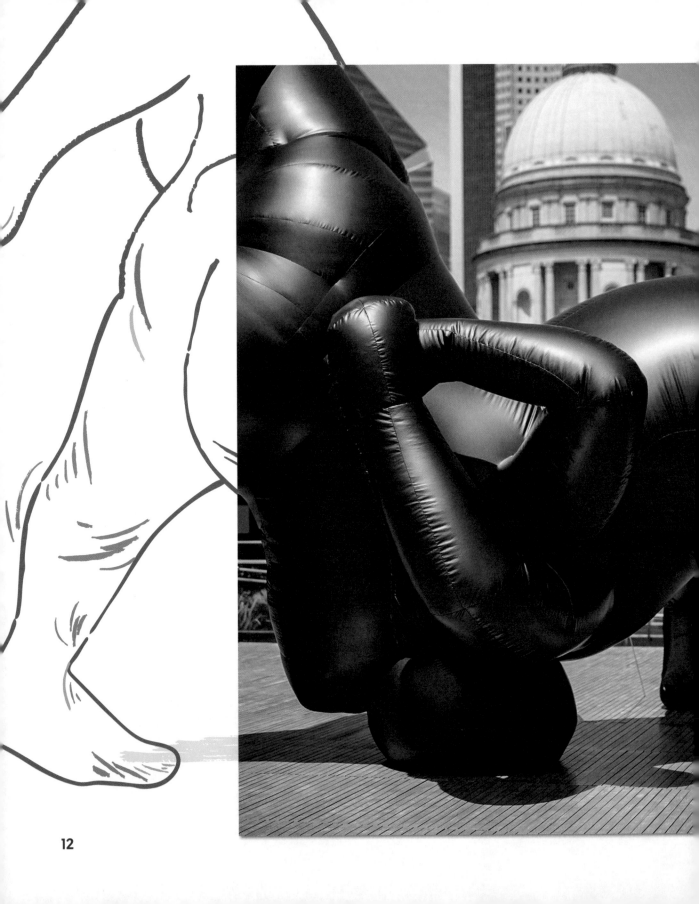

What do you notice
about the sculpture?

Shilpa Gupta, *Untitled* (2023). Inflatable. 650 × 480 × 518 cm.
Photo by Joseph Nair, Memphis West.
Commissioned by National Gallery Singapore

Do you notice that it has two bodies and one head? What do you think it could be about?

The answer is printed at the bottom of the page in reverse.

THE SCULPTURE IS ABOUT CONFLICTING FEELINGS THAT WE EXPERIENCE INSIDE OUR HEAD AS WELL AS CONTRASTING EXPERIENCES OUTSIDE OF OURSELVES IN OUR SURROUNDINGS.

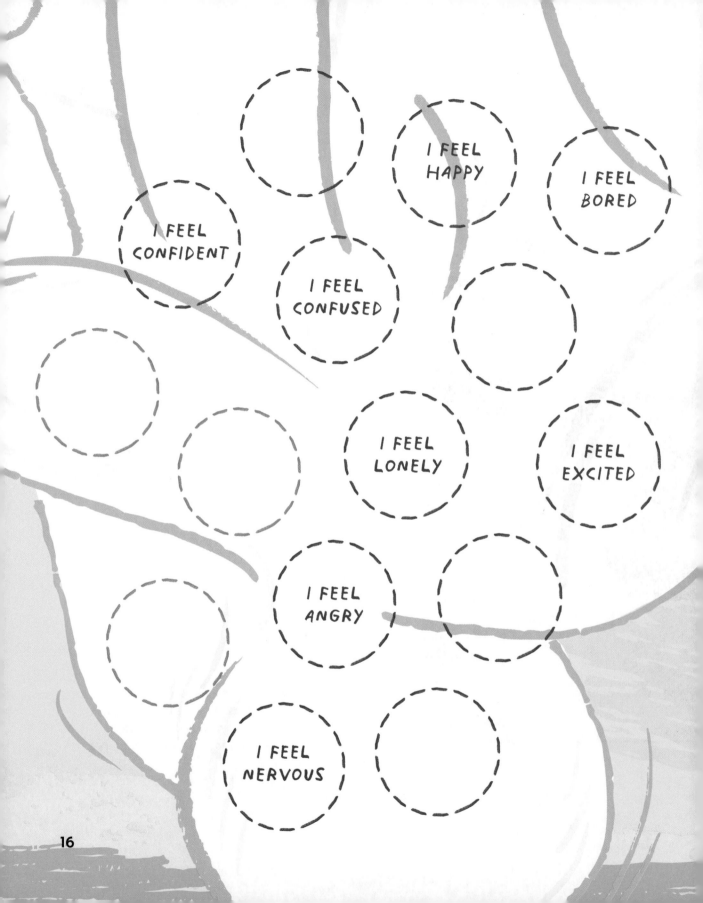

16

What are the feelings you feel sometimes? Write, circle, colour or draw them inside the body of the sculpture.

Sometimes we feel happy and excited about something, like when our friends come to our birthday party! We can also feel sad and disappointed at the same time because one of our best friends is sick and can't make it. Such contradictory feelings! We are both happy and sad. Have you ever had two conflicting feelings at the same time?

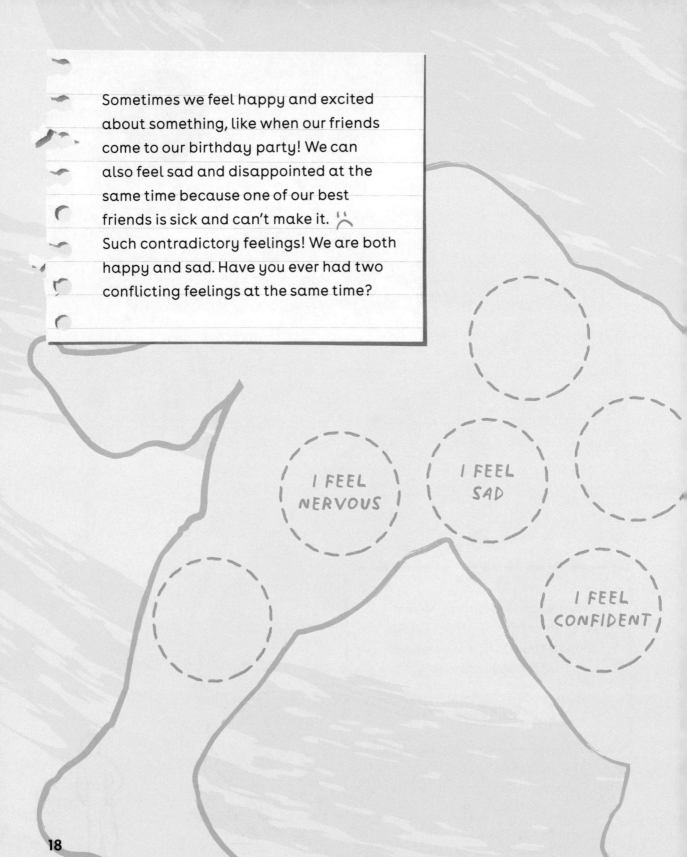

I FEEL NERVOUS

I FEEL SAD

I FEEL CONFIDENT

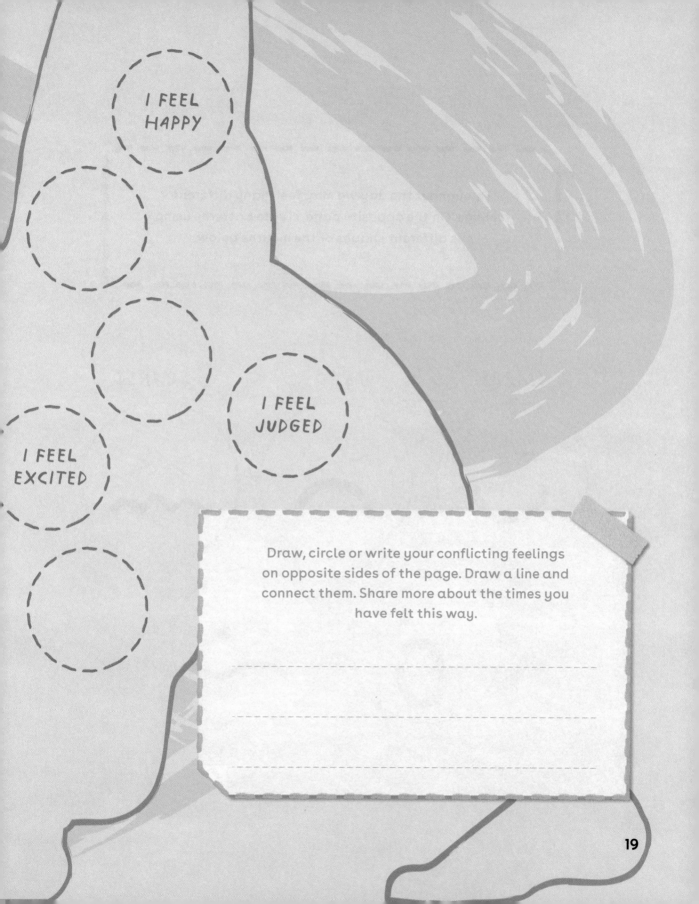

I FEEL
HAPPY

I FEEL
JUDGED

I FEEL
EXCITED

Draw, circle or write your conflicting feelings
on opposite sides of the page. Draw a line and
connect them. Share more about the times you
have felt this way.

Throughout the day we may feel many different feelings. On the opposite page, create patterns using the different shapes of the mouths below.

HAPPY   SAD   SCARED

SHOCKED   ANGRY

Create your
pattern here!

Sometimes when I meet new people,
I feel nervous and scared inside, but
I smile at people and talk a lot. This
makes me look happy on the outside,
but that is not how what I feel inside.
Do you ever appear one way on the
outside and another way inside?

Draw or write what you
feel on the **inside**.

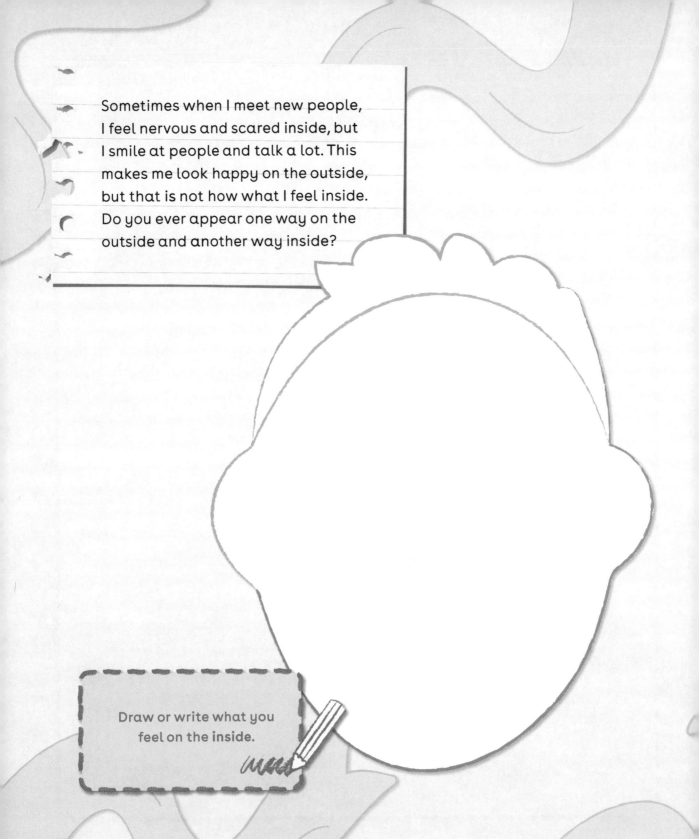

When we show people a different feeling than the one we're feeling inside, we can describe that as **"wearing a mask"**. There are many types of masks that we can wear.

OUR INNER WORLDS

OUR OUTER WORLDS

Draw or write what you show on the outside.

We may feel nervous about our first day at school or work because we don't know anyone and we may put on **"a brave mask"** to help us meet people and make friends. That mask may look like a smile when we feel like crying, or may sound like speaking differently to help us fit in.

23

DID YOU KNOW?

Many writers wear "masks" to hide their true identities to publish their books. There are many famous writers who have written by using a fake name! They did so because they wanted to write freely and not be restricted by the expectations of others.

Author of the famous thriller *The Stranger Beside Me*, **Anne Rule** was told by her editor to hide her gender when writing crime novels.

Nobel Prize winner **Pablo Neruda** from South America took on a fake name as he thought his father would not approve of his poems!

The English author **Emily Bronte** wrote under a gender-neutral name Ellis Bell to publish books.

If you were to write a book under a fake name, what would it be about? Imagine and create your book cover here!

TITLE OF YOUR IMAGINARY BOOK

YOUR CHOSEN PSEUDONYM/ FAKE NAME

STORY OF YOUR BOOK IN A FEW LINES

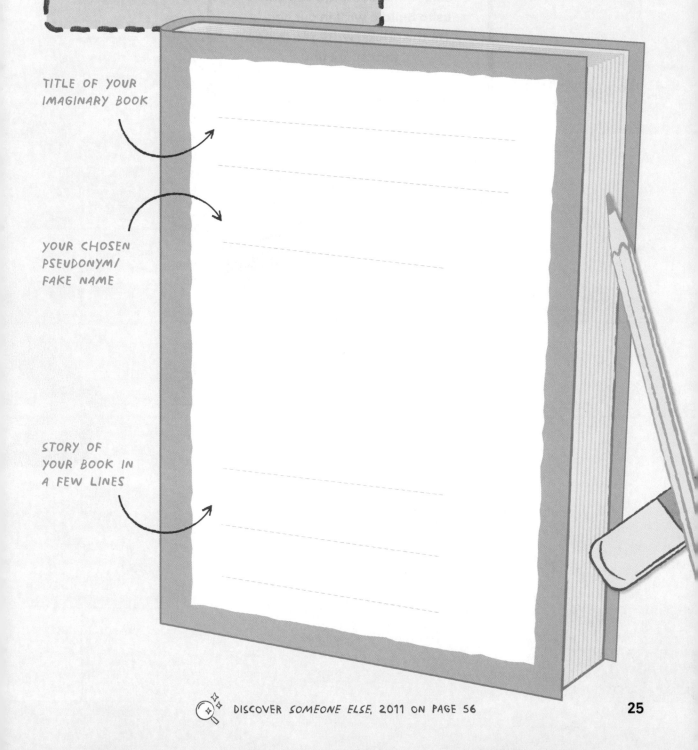

DISCOVER *SOMEONE ELSE*, 2011 ON PAGE 56

Sometimes our fears can cause us to build a wall in our heads. On the bricks, write the things that scare you.

What helps you overcome your fear and break through these walls? Write or draw the actions, people, or things that help you feel less scared.

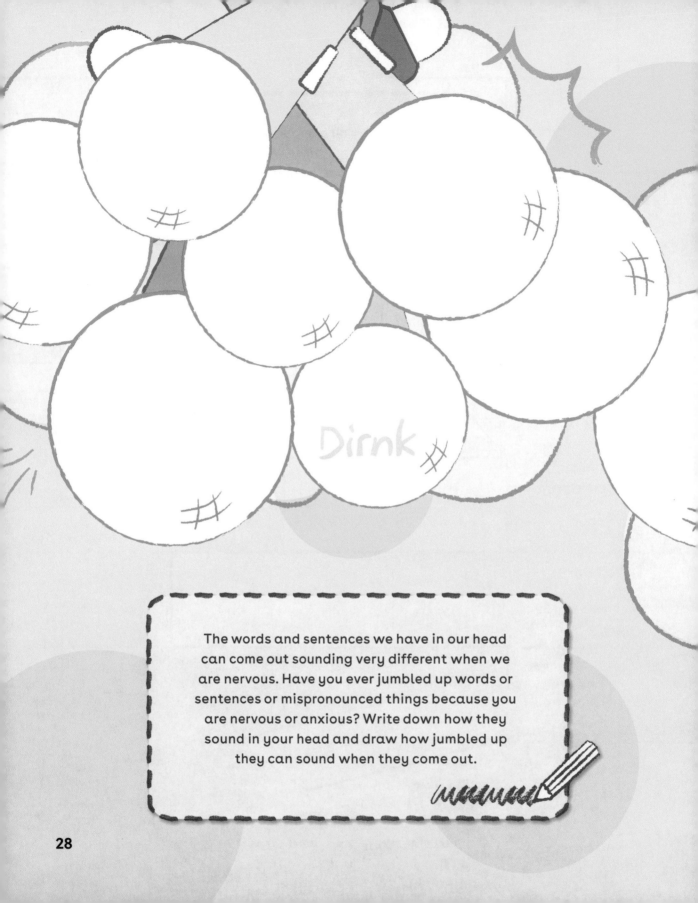

Dirnk

The words and sentences we have in our head can come out sounding very different when we are nervous. Have you ever jumbled up words or sentences or mispronounced things because you are nervous or anxious? Write down how they sound in your head and draw how jumbled up they can sound when they come out.

DISCOVER *SINGING CLOUD*, 2008–2009 ON PAGE 57

There are so many things around us that we may struggle to understand—often just because they are different from us or how we do our things. Somebody eats food with chopsticks, someone else eats food with a spoon and someone else eats with their hands! Or someone around us has eyes different from us, someone has different skin colour or someone else speaks a different language or wears different clothes or might go to a different place of worship.

It makes it interesting that we have so many differences! Write down the things you enjoy and appreciate, as well as those you don't understand or feel confused or curious about, whether they are about your friends, your neighbourhood or the world beyond!

MY FRIENDS

OUR INNER WORLDS

OUR OUTER WORLDS

MY NEIGHBOURHOOD

THE WORLD

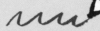

WHEREDOIENDANDYOUBEGIN

Make a collage using newspapers, magazines and books. Look for the letters in *Wheredoiendandyoubegin*. Cut the letters out and stick them along the dotted line to create your own version.

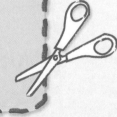

DISCOVER *WHEREDOIENDANDYOUBEGIN*, 2012 ON PAGE 57

Trace, colour and cut along the lines and interweave the four different languages together using string. There are some extra blank templates available. Ask your parents, grandparents, friends or neighbours to write "We Change Each Other" in other languages—each word per designated area. Add this to your bunting.

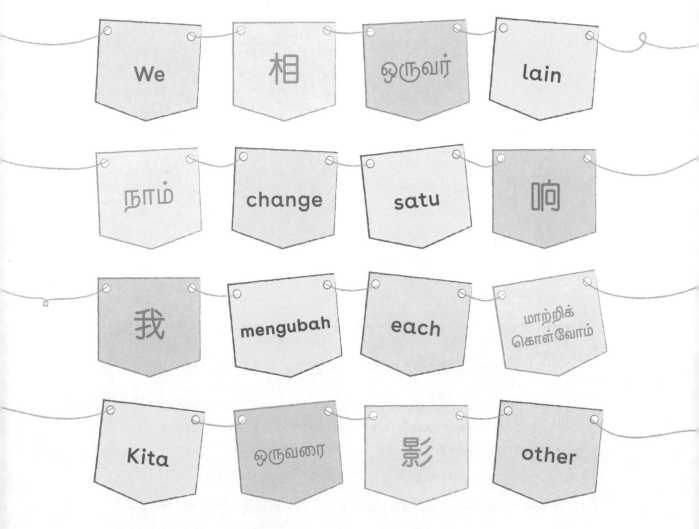

We | 相 | ஒருவர் | lain

நாம் | change | satu | 响

我 | mengubah | each | மாற்றிக் கொள்வோம்

Kita | ஒருவரை | 影 | other

DISCOVER *WE CHANGE EACH OTHER*, 2017 ON PAGE 58

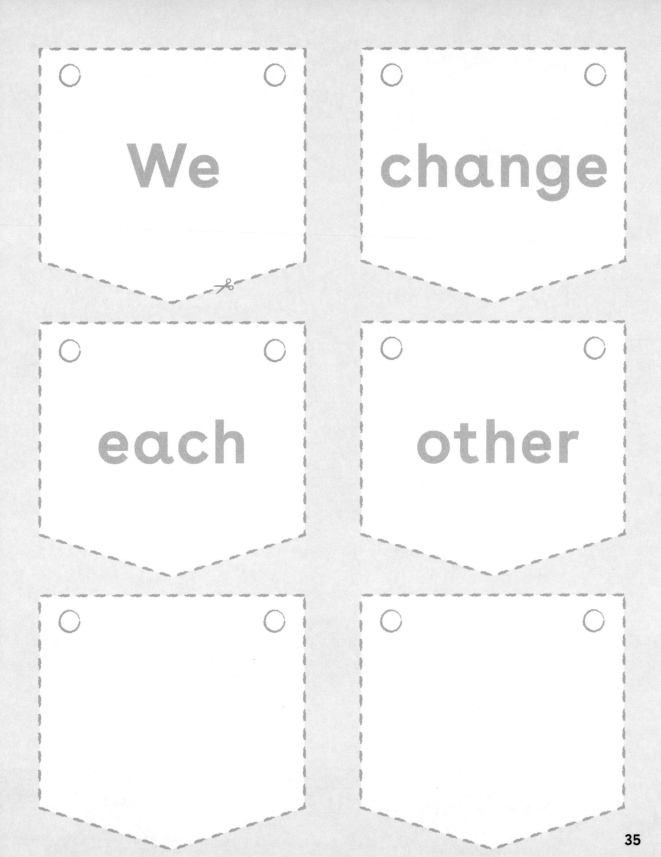

We

change

each

other

38

நாம்

ஒருவரை

ஒருவர்

மாற்றிக்
கொள்வோம்

39

40

Kita

mengubah

satu

sama

lain

Sometimes my feelings can get so big that I need to release them either by talking to someone who cares about me or by moving my body. What do you do when your feelings feel like they get too big?

Trace your left hand on the opposite page and trace your right hand on this page. Write what makes you happy on your left hand. Write what makes you sad on your right hand.

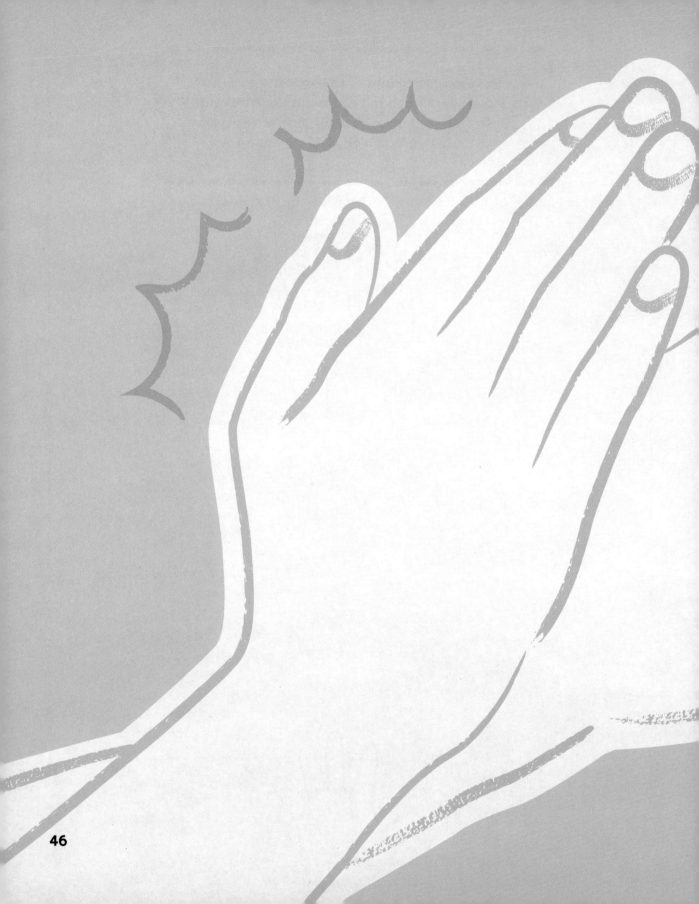

OUR
BODIES IN
ACTION

Take your happy hand and your sad hand and clap them together. Clap out a sad rhythm. Clap out a happy rhythm. Colour how your hands feel after releasing both these feelings.

47

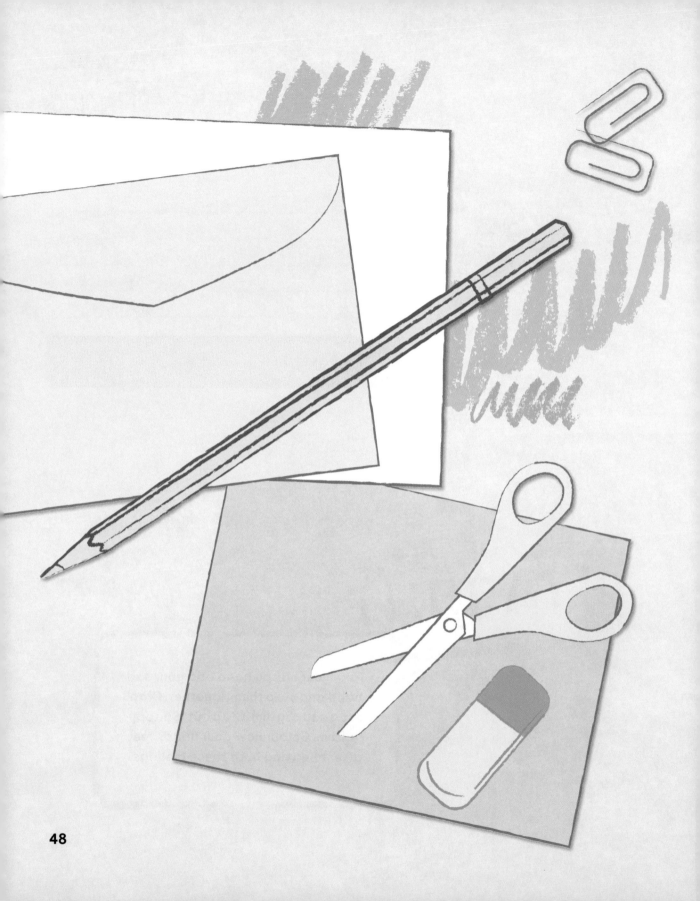

Write to a friend or family member or to yourself about a time you felt two conflicting feelings at the same time.

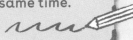

DISCOVER *UNTITLED*, 1995-96 ON PAGE 58

TO

PleASE- DispOSe -
AfTeR - USe -

Feelings aren't good or bad. They point us in the direction of where we need to look after ourselves or they bring attention to the things we enjoy. The stories and messages that we attach to these feelings are what cause conflict. On the balloons, write or draw a message about your feelings that you want to release.

DISCOVER *I WANT TO LIVE WITH NO FEAR*, 2010 ON PAGE 59

We're so glad we could go on this journey
of art and our feelings together.

Getting to know our conflicting feelings and
learning to be curious about other people's
differences have made it a little bit easier
to have more space for ourselves and others.

Thank you for joining us!

SHILPA & ROSIE

Dear Parents and Teachers,

In this resource, you'll find a gentle guide to help support you or the young people you're working with, as well as possible questions you can ask yourself or these same young people to deepen your connection to the artivities you're doing. Take what you need and leave the rest behind.

As you do the artivities, we encourage you to allow and notice what may be coming up for you and the young people you're working with. Let's aim to create a space that allows for reflection and process, a space that allows them to be brave enough to share their feelings with you and where you are able to truly hear what they are saying.

There's no need to solve any problems here! You don't need to fix or change anything. Just offer support if and when needed and be present to how they are feeling.

Look out for their body language, their tone of voice as well as what they are saying.

Ask open ended questions that follow up with what has been said or that can clarify things you are unsure about. Listen to understand where they are coming from, as opposed to listening to share your opinion or to validate your experiences.

Be mindful about your own body language, as well as your tone of voice and the words you are using. Check in with your breath, take deep breaths if needed and ground yourself if you notice you are very upset or bothered by something.

We encourage you to use Rosie's new five Cs—Communicate Clearly with Care, Compassion and Curiosity.

Thank you for being willing to go on this journey of exploration and discovery with the young person (or people) you are with.

LET'S GO DEEPER

Our Inner Worlds

Our Inner/ Outer Worlds

Our Outer Worlds

Our Bodies in Action

LET'S FIND OUT MORE ABOUT SHILPA'S ART

Someone Else—A library of 100 books written anonymously or under pseudonyms, 2011. Etched metal books, 488 × 22 × 190 cm. Photo by Anil Rane.

Someone Else

In *Someone Else*, we see 100 metal books neatly stacked on shelves. If you look closely, you discover that the author's name on each book isn't real. It's a made-up name and there's a reason why. It's like a mystery game because you can't see the author's real self, just their book cover. The artist wants us to think about why people use fake names. Is it because they're scared or want to hide a part of themselves? Some authors used fake names to hide their gender. Some didn't want their families to know they were writers. Others just wanted to write in a language they really liked.

Threat

Threat is a sculpture made from soap bars, each bar with the word "THREAT" carved on it. The sculpture makes you think about how things that seem harmless can sometimes seem scary. You could even take a bar of soap and as you use it, you could think about how some threats aren't real. When we use the soap, the word "threat" starts to fade away and disappear, showing how we can make scary things go away by talking about them or working together with others. In a way, it's like washing away our fears.

Threat, 2008–09. Bathing Soap, 15 × 6.2 × 4 cm each. Photo by Didier Bamoso.

Singing Cloud

Imagine *Singing Cloud* as a huge thing that's part cloud, part creature, suspended in the space—it is covered with more than 4,000 microphones. Its entire skin seems to start speaking to us. That is because the microphones are rewired and they contain speakers instead. The sounds they make are like a magical choir with hypnotic speech fragments. These voices float through a dimly lit gallery, carrying voices of people across places and through time; their intertwined histories and deep human desires that seek to be free.

Singing Cloud, 2008–09. Object built with thousands of microphones with multi-channel audio; 9min 30sec audio loop, 457 × 61 × 152 cm. Commissioned by Le Laboratoire, Paris. Photo by Marc Domage.

Wheredolendandyoubegin

Wheredolendandyoubegin is a light artwork that can take different shapes—it can be a straight line or even form a circle. When it gets dark, the artwork glows softly and makes us think about how we're all connected. The words and texts in the artwork come together, like two people holding hands. It could be a mom and a child, two friends or even neighbours living next door to each other. They're all sharing the same sky above them. This artwork shows us how borders and boundaries, like the sky, can't keep us apart. It reminds us of a place where there are no divisions based on things like religion, race or country.

Wheredolendandyoubegin, 2012. LED-based light installation, 800 × 68 cm. Commissioned by Beppu Contemporary Art Festival 2012. Photo by Hendrik Zeitler.

We Change Each Other

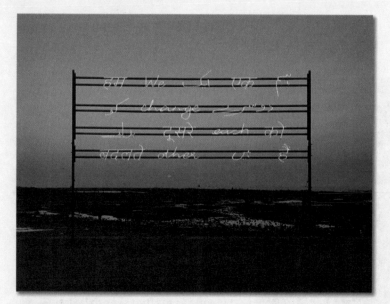

In this animated light artwork, the phrase "We Change Each Other" appears in three different languages, interwoven into each other. It's like words start on lines of a notebook, forming a continuous sentence where these languages mix and overlap. Only one language lights up at a time, reminding us to notice the "Other." The sentence is broken up on purpose to show how change and mixing happen when different people or cultures meet.

We Change Each Other, 2017. Animated outdoor light installation, 222 × 189 inches.

Untitled

In *Untitled*, the artist posted 300 ink drawings anonymously to strangers, whose names were randomly taken from a public art gallery's mailing list. Each drawing had three numbers on it: one for that drawing itself, one for the drawing before it and one for a future drawing. People received the artwork in their mail, amongst their regular mail, arriving unexpectedly like a gift. There were no names on them, just a stamp that said, "Please dispose after use." This early work, which was made in the mid-1990s, sets out some of the artist's continuing interests—time, measurement, and the blurring of boundaries.

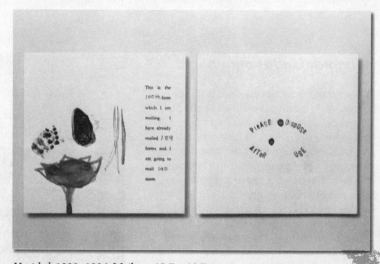

Untitled, 1995–1996. Mail art, 12.7 × 12.7 cm.